27/8/10
28/9/11
M-A

2 4 SEP

Mob
the
Runaway Train

Roger Hurn

Illustrated by
Stik

RISING★STARS

Rising Stars UK Ltd.
22 Grafton Street, London W1S 4EX
www.risingstars-uk.com

The right of Roger Hurn to be identified as the author of this work
has been asserted by him in accordance with the Copyright,
Design and Patents Act 1988.

Published 2008

Text, design and layout © Rising Stars UK Ltd.

Cover design: Burville-Riley Partnership
Illustrator: Stik, Bill Greenhead for Illustration Ltd
Text design and typesetting: Andy Wilson
Publisher: Gill Budgell
Editor: Catherine Baker

British Library Cataloguing in Publication Data.
A CIP record for this book is available from the British Library

ISBN: 978-1-84680-431-1

Printed in the UK by CPI Bookmarque, Croydon, CR0 4TD

Mixed Sources
Product group from well-managed
forests and other controlled sources
www.fsc.org Cert no. TT-COC-002227
© 1996 Forest Stewardship Council
FSC

Contents

Meet the Mystery Mob   4

Chapter 1: Watch Out! There's
        a Spy About   7

Chapter 2: An Inspector Calls   13

Chapter 3: Gum Rushes In   20

Chapter 4: It's a Knock-out   25

Chapter 5: A Close Call   30

Extras!

About the author   39
Railway quiz   40
When I was a kid   42
Adi's favourite train joke   43
How to be a trainspotter   44
Five fantastic facts about trains   46
Train lingo   47

Meet the Mystery Mob

Name:

Gummy

FYI: Gummy hasn't got much brain – and even fewer teeth.

Loves: Soup.

Hates: Toffee chews.

Fact: The brightest thing about him is his shirt.

Name:

Lee

FYI: If Lee was any cooler he'd be a cucumber.

Loves: Hip-hop.

Hates: Hopscotch.

Fact: He has his own designer label (which he peeled off a tin).

Name:

FYI: Rob lives in his own world – he's just visiting planet Earth.

Loves: Daydreaming.

Hates: Nightmares.

Fact: Rob always does his homework – he just forgets to write it down.

Name:

Dwayne

FYI: Dwayne is smarter than a tree full of owls.

Loves: Anything complicated.

Hates: Join-the-dots books.

Fact: If he was any brighter you could use him as a floodlight at football matches.

Name:

Chet

FYI: Chet is as brave as a lion with steel jaws.

Loves: Having adventures.

Hates: Knitting.

Fact: He's as tough as the chicken his granny cooks for his tea.

Name:

Adi

FYI: Adi is as happy as a football fan with tickets to the big match.

Loves: Telling jokes.

Hates: Moaning minnies.

Fact: He knows more jokes than a jumbo joke book.

Watch Out!
There's a Spy About

The Mystery Mob are on a train
going to London. The only other
person in the carriage is a man
with a briefcase. He's reading
the newspaper. Then another man
comes in. He's wearing a big black
hat, dark glasses and a long mac.
He squeezes into a seat. The train
goes into a tunnel, and suddenly
all the lights go out!

Gummy   What's going on? Who's turned the lights off?! I can't see a thing!

Dwayne   Oh, take a chill pill, Gummy. The lights'll come back on in a moment.

But when the lights come back on, the man in the hat has gone.

Reading man

Help! My briefcase has been stolen!

Dwayne That bloke in the hat must have taken it.

Gummy What's in it – your packed lunch?

Man No, I'm a scientist and my top-secret plans for a new deep space rocket are in that briefcase. I must get them back!

Dwayne Wow! So that other guy is a spy. Cool!

Man   No, it's not cool. He's getting
away with my briefcase
and I'll be in real trouble
if I don't get those plans back.

Gummy   Don't panic. We're the Mystery
Mob. Catching bad guys
is what we do. We'll find that spy
and rescue the top-secret plans
for you.

Dwayne   That's right. Okay, listen up,
you guys. This train is going
way too fast for the spy
to jump off. He must still be
on board.

Gummy   Okay, we'll split up and see
if we can track him down.
But let's be quick about it –
I haven't had my sandwiches yet!

Dwayne   Lee, you and Rob can check out
the back of the train.

Lee and Rob give Dwayne the thumbs up.

Gummy   (eagerly) Can we check the buffet car?

Dwayne   No, that's Chet and Adi's job. If I let you go in the buffet car you'd look for a pie, not a spy!

Gummy   Doh!

Dwayne   So we're going to check out the front of the train.

The boys race off, while the rocket scientist phones the police on his mobile phone.

②

An Inspector Calls

As they head for the front of the train, Gummy sees someone in a black hat nipping into the toilet.

Gummy   Hey, Dwayne. I think I spotted the spy going into the loo.

Dwayne   Are you sure?

Gummy   Yep.

Dwayne So what's he doing in there?

Gummy He's probably going to the loo, Dwayne.

Dwayne (groaning) No, you dummy. I mean, perhaps he's hiding the top-secret plans!

Gummy Oh, I get you. Well, we'll nab him when he comes out and then we'll see.

Dwayne Right. Let's grab this first-aid blanket and throw it over the spy as soon as he opens the loo door.

Gummy Great idea!

The toilet door opens and someone in a black hat steps out. Gummy and Dwayne jump on him with the blanket. The man falls to the floor.

TOILE

Dwayne   Well done, Gum. We've got him.

Gummy   Right. Let's see who he is.

They pull the blanket off the man.
He sits up and glares at them.
He is not the spy.

Dwayne   Whoops!

Gummy   We thought you were a spy.

Dwayne   No, Gummy, *you* thought
he was a spy.

Gummy   Well, he *is* wearing a black hat.

Dwayne   Yes, but it says 'ticket inspector'
on it. It's part of his uniform!

Gummy   (gulping) Please don't look
at me like that, Mr Ticket
Inspector. I have got a ticket,
honest.

Ticket Inspector

(angrily) Never mind about a
ticket. You two have got some
explaining to do.

Dwayne Sorry, but we don't have time
to explain. We've got a spy to
track down. Come on, Gum.
Let's go.

Ticket Inspector

Oi! You come back with that
blanket!

Gummy Here, Mr Ticket Inspector, catch!

Gummy throws the blanket to the ticket inspector. The blanket lands on his head. Now the Ticket Inspector can't see where he's going. By the time he gets free of the blanket, Dwayne and Gummy have gone.

3

Gum Rushes In

Dwayne and Gummy go up to the front of the train. The front carriage is empty but they can see the spy is in the driver's cab.

Dwayne Look! There's the spy.

Gummy But what's he doing?

Dwayne (sighing) Gummy, I expect
he wants to make the driver stop
the train so he can escape.

Gummy   Ah, right. Sorry.

Dwayne   And from the way he's shaking
his fist and the driver's
shaking his head, I guess
the driver's saying no.

Gummy The spy's getting really cross.

Dwayne Yes. Come on. We've got to do something to help.

Gummy Well, what are we waiting for? Let's go in the cab and grab that spy.

Dwayne Right.

Gummy No, wait. I bet the cab door's locked.

Dwayne Er … I don't think it is, 'cos …

Gummy   No problem. I'll bash the door
down with my shoulder like
the cops do on TV.

Dwayne   No – wait, Gum. Let's try
the door handle first.

Gummy   There's no time for that.
Out of my way, Dwayne!

Gummy runs at the door. He bounces
back off it. The door doesn't budge.

Gummy   (rubbing his shoulder)
Ooooohhhh! That hurts.

Dwayne Right. Now for Plan B. I'll try the door handle. Oh look. It works! The door's not locked after all. That's how the spy got in.

Gummy Now you tell me!

Dwayne Hey, the spy looks like he's going to thump the driver!

Gummy Don't worry. I'll soon fix him.

But how will Gummy fix the spy? He has enough trouble just opening a door.

4

It's a Knock-Out

Gummy and Dwayne burst into the cab.
The spy is so surprised to see them
that he does a double take.

Spy   What do you two kids think
            you're doing?

Gummy   We're going to stop you
            from stealing the top-secret plans.

Spy   You're too late. I've already
            stolen them.

Dwayne   Yes, what my friend means
is that we're going to stop you
from escaping with them.

Spy   You've got no chance.
I'll just finish off this driver
and then I'll deal with you two!

The spy rushes at the driver with his
fists up. Then Dwayne sees something.

Dwayne (whispering) Look, Gum! The spy's dropped the briefcase on the floor.

Gummy Great! That's just what I need.

Gummy grabs the heavy briefcase and swings it round his head.

Dwayne Don't go mad with that heavy case, Gum! You'll hit the driver as well. Doh! Too late!

Gummy loses his balance. The briefcase whacks the spy and the train driver. They are both knocked out cold.

Gummy   Hey, I showed that spy who's the boss around here.

Dwayne   True, but you got the driver too.

Gummy   I didn't mean to, but at least we've got the top-secret plans back.

Dwayne   We have. And we've also got a runaway train.

Gummy   What are you on about?

Dwayne   (yelling) Gummy, the train
is speeding out of control
and we don't know how to stop it!

Gummy   Calm down, Dwayne!
The driver does.

Dwayne   Yes, but sadly for us, you knocked
the driver out. So unless I can
think of something fast,
we've had it!

A Close Call

Dwayne and Gummy stare at the control panel. There are two levers. One is red and one is green.

Gummy   What are these two levers for, Dwayne?

Dwayne   Well, I guess one is the throttle and one is the brake.

Gummy   Yeah, I'd figured that out. But which one is which?

Dwayne   I really don't know. I'm going to have to think about it.

Dwayne strokes his chin and frowns
as he stares at the levers. Gummy looks
out of the train window. He does
a double take.

Gummy   I hate to bother you when you're
thinking, Dwayne.

Dwayne   Then don't.

Gummy   Okay, but there's something
you need to know.

Dwayne (crossly) What is it?

Gummy There's a level crossing ahead of us. The gates are closed across the track and the signal is red. I think we're going to crash.

Dwayne I don't believe it. Surely things can't get any worse.

Gummy Oh yes they can. I forgot to tell you that there's a coach going over the crossing.

Dwayne Right. I've made up my mind.
Pull the lever on the left. Quick!

Gummy I'm doing it!

Gummy pulls on the lever. The runaway
train screeches to a stop just in front
of the gates.

Dwayne Phew! Well done, Gum.

Gummy   You're such a brain box,
Dwayne. How did you know
which was the right lever?

Dwayne   I didn't.

Gummy   What? Do you mean it was just
a lucky guess?

Dwayne   No, it was an educated guess.
I'm a brain box, remember?
You see, the stop signal was red
so I figured the red lever
must be the brake.

Gummy   And you were right!

Dwayne   Luckily.

Gummy   But you just said – oh,
never mind.

The spy groans and sits up. His hat
falls off. Long blonde hair spills out.

Dwayne   Hey! Our spy is a woman.

Gummy   Wow. She fooled me.
I thought our spy was a guy!

The rocket scientist and a policeman
come into the cab.

Scientist   Well done, boys. This is Ila
Nockitoff, the top spy.
But, thanks to you two,
her spying days are over.
Come on, Ila, you're going
to jail!

The policeman takes Ila away.

Gummy   That spy didn't stand a chance against us, Dwayne.

Dwayne   That's right. She'd have to be smarter than James Bond to get the better of you and me, Gummy.

Gummy   I always knew I could be the next James Bond.

Dwayne   Really? How come?

Gummy   'Cos when we play I Spy
I always win!

Dwayne   Yes, but only if you're
spying food.

Gummy   Good point. And I think
I'll do some more spying right
now. See you.

Dwayne   Hey, where are you going?

Gummy   To the buffet car. I'm starving!

About
the author

Roger Hurn has:

- had a hit record in Turkey
- won *The Weakest Link* on TV
- swum with sharks on the Great Barrier Reef.

Now he's a writer, and he hopes you like reading about the Mystery Mob as much as he likes writing about them.

The railway quiz

Questions

1 What did the monster say when he saw a rush-hour train full of passengers?

2 What is evil and ugly and goes at 125 mph?

3 What do you get when you cross an alligator and a railway track?

4 Why don't elephants like to ride on trains?

5 Where do ghost trains stop?

6 Why did the boy who did a project on trains find it hard?

7 Why isn't it safe to doze on trains?

8 Why do you have to wait so long for a ghost train to come along?

Answers

1 Yummy! A chew-chew train!
2 A monster in a high-speed train.
3 Three pieces of alligator!
4 Because they hate leaving their trunks in the baggage car!
5 At devil crossings!
6 He had to keep track of everything!
7 They run over sleepers!
8 They only run a skeleton service!

How did you score?

👋 If you got all eight railway answers correct, then it's full steam ahead for you.

👋 If you got six railway answers correct, then you are on the right track.

👋 If you got fewer than four railway answers correct, then you are definitely coming off the rails!

When I was a kid

Question Did you like riding on trains when you were a kid?

Roger Yes, but I nearly got into trouble once.

Question Why?

Roger Well, the ticket inspector was asking to see everyone's ticket. I looked everywhere for mine. I looked in my pockets and in my bag.

Question Where was your ticket?

Roger It was sticking out of my mouth!

Question Doh! What did the inspector do?

Roger He snatched it out of my mouth, clipped it and gave it back to me. Then he walked away laughing.

Question Didn't you feel really silly?

Roger No. The joke was on him.

Question How come?

Roger I'd been chewing the date off my ticket!

Adi's favourite train joke

What's the difference between a teacher and a steam train?

A teacher says, 'Spit your gum out,' and a steam train says, 'Choo, choo, choo'!

How to be a trainspotter

1. It's easy to spot a train – they're those great big metal things that run on railway tracks and make a lot of noise.

2. *Trains are not shy woodland creatures – just go to your local railway station and you'll soon spot loads.*

3. Never buy a cup of tea or coffee at the station – always bring your own hot drinks with you in a large thermos flask.

4. *Never buy food at the station – always take doorstep-sized sandwiches wrapped up in greaseproof paper.*

5 Note down the numbers of the trains you spot in a tatty old notebook. Only show-offs use a clipboard.

6 *Always wear an anorak and bobble hat even on the hottest day. And make sure your anorak has plenty of pockets for your thermos flask, sandwiches, notebook, pencils, leaky biros, other pencils, more pencils, boiled sweets, old sweet wrappers etc.*

Five fantastic facts about trains

1   The first passenger railway line in the world
    was the Stockton and Darlington Railway,
    built in 1825.

2   The first locomotive to pull a passenger train
    was *Locomotion*. It was built, in England
    by George Stephenson.

3   In 1829, *Rocket* was the world's
    fastest train with a top speed of 36 miles
    (58 km) per hour. Many people believed
    that travelling at that speed could kill you.

4   In fact, the first person to die in a railway
    accident was William Huskisson in 1830,
    and it wasn't speed that killed him
    but carelessness. He accidentally stepped
    in front of *Rocket*.

5   Today the fastest train in the world
    is the TGV in France. It has a top speed
    of 357 miles per hour – ten times faster
    than *Rocket*.

Train lingo

Anorak Not a waterproof coat, but the name for a person who likes to go trainspotting.

Buffer The two metal discs on springs at the end of the railway line that reduce the shock when a train hits them.

Gripper A ticket inspector. If you don't have a ticket he'll try to get a grip on you!

John Wayne Cockney rhyming slang for train – e.g. 'I'm catching the John Wayne'.

Photter Someone whose hobby is photographing trains. Any photter with the name Harry probably thinks trains are magic.

Sleeper The wooden brace between the railway tracks. Not someone in the land of dreams.

Mystery Mob

Mystery Mob Set 1:

Mystery Mob and the Abominable Snowman
Mystery Mob and the Big Match
Mystery Mob and the Circus of Doom
Mystery Mob and the Creepy Castle
Mystery Mob and the Haunted Attic
Mystery Mob and the Hidden Treasure
Mystery Mob and the Magic Bottle
Mystery Mob and the Missing Millions
Mystery Mob and the Monster on the Moor
Mystery Mob and the Mummy's Curse
Mystery Mob and the Time Machine
Mystery Mob and the UFO

Mystery Mob Set 2:

Mystery Mob and the Ghost Town
Mystery Mob and the Bonfire Night Plot
Mystery Mob and the April Fools' Day Joker
Mystery Mob and the Great Pancake Day Race
Mystery Mob and the Scary Santa
Mystery Mob and the Conker Conspiracy
Mystery Mob and the Top Talent Contest
Mystery Mob and the Night in the Waxworks
Mystery Mob and the Runaway Train
Mystery Mob and the Wrong Robot
Mystery Mob and the Day of the Dinosaurs
Mystery Mob and the Man-eating Tiger

RISING★STARS

Mystery Mob books are available from most booksellers.

**For mail order information
please call Rising Stars on 0871 47 23 010
or visit www.risingstars-uk.com**